We Live in North America

by Susan Ring

Consultant: Dwight Herold, Ed.D., Past President,
Iowa Council for the Social Studies

Yellow
Umbrella
Books
for early readers

Yellow Umbrella Books are published by Red Brick Learning
7825 Telegraph Road, Bloomington, Minnesota 55438
http://www.redbricklearning.com

Editorial Director: Mary Lindeen
Senior Editor: Hollie J. Endres
Senior Designer and Illustrator: Gene Bentdahl
Photo Researcher: Signature Design
Developer: Raindrop Publishing
Consultant: Dwight Herold, Ed.D., Past President, Iowa Council for the Social Studies
Conversion Assistants: Jenny Marks, Laura Manthe

Library of Congress Cataloging-in-Publication Data
Ring, Susan
  We Live in North America / by Susan Ring
     p. cm.
  Includes index.
  ISBN 0-7368-5845-8 (hardcover)
  ISBN 0-7368-5275-1 (softcover)
  1. North America—Juvenile literature. I. Title. II. Series.
  E38.5.R56 2005
  970—dc22
                                        2005016154

Photo Credits:
Cover: Corel; Title Page and Page 2: Corbis; Page 3: Lindsay Hebberd/Corbis; Page 4: Corel;
(inset) Jupiter Images; Page 5: Corel; Page 6: Johnathan Hayward; CP/AP/Wide World Photos;
Page 7: Jupiter Images; Page 8: Randy Faris/Corbis; Page 9: Ellis Neel; Alamogordo Daily
News/AP/Wide World Photos; Page 10: William Bernard/Corbis; Page 11: Corel; Page 12:
Corel ; Page 13: Hemera Photo Objects

1 2 3 4 5 6 11 10 09 08 07 06

Table of Contents

A Big Land

We live in North America. North America is a **continent**. It spreads far and wide. North America is made up of big countries and small island nations. Canada, Mexico, and the United States are the largest countries in North America.

These three countries are different from each other in many ways. Each has its own history and holidays. Each has its own cities and towns. Yet these three countries share some things, too. Let's take a closer look at this big land we call North America.

Canada

Welcome to Canada! Canada is the second-largest country in the world. It is a land of snowy mountains and blue lakes. Canada has many forests. The forests are home to bears, wolves, and moose. Northern Canada is very close to the North Pole.

Ottawa is Canada's **capital**. It is a big and busy city. Ottawa has many museums. All over Canada you can hear people speak English. Many people in Canada also speak French.

Let's celebrate! July 1st is **Canada Day**. It celebrates an important day in Canadian history. This is the day in 1867 when Canada became a nation. People have picnics and march in parades. These children are proudly waving Canada's flag.

Mexico

Mexico is a land of hot deserts and cool mountains. People also like to visit its sandy beaches by the ocean. Mexico has rain forests that are filled with many different kinds of plants and animals.

Mexico City is Mexico's capital. Mexico City is one of the biggest cities in the world. It has both new buildings and old churches. A very large square is at the heart of the city. People in all of Mexico speak Spanish.

Cinco de Mayo means May 5th in Spanish. That's when people celebrate this **festive** Mexican holiday. People dance, sing, and eat traditional food. Cinco de Mayo celebrates a battle that Mexico won in 1862.

The United States

The United States has places that are hot and places that are covered in snow. It has green forests and dry deserts. All kinds of animals live in the United States. Alligators swim in the warm rivers. Mountain lions make their homes on rocky cliffs.

Washington, D.C., is the country's capital. Many visitors come to see the buildings and **monuments** there. Most people in the United States speak English. You can hear many other languages being spoken almost anywhere you go.

Here comes a marching band! It's the Fourth of July. That's when Americans celebrate Independence Day. People wave the flag and march in parades. Many people have picnics. At night people watch colorful fireworks.

One Land, Many People

Canada, Mexico, and the United States are three different countries. Each one has its special holidays and foods. Each one has its own flag and its own history. They share some things in common, as well.

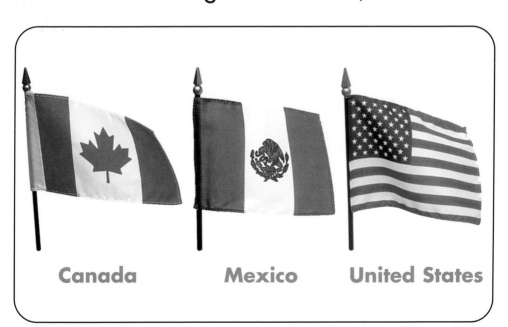

Canada   Mexico   United States

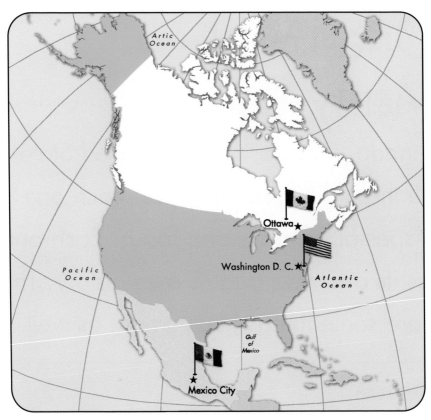

These three countries share mountain ranges and huge lakes. They share waterfalls, rivers, and oceans. And of course, all three countries share one land with many people. They share North America.

Glossary

Canada Day—Canadian holiday that celebrates becoming a nation

capital—the city where people in a country's government work

Cinco de Mayo—Mexican holiday that celebrates winning a battle

continent—large land mass made up of different countries

festive—happy and merry

Fourth of July—holiday in the United States that celebrates becoming a nation

monument—a building or statue that honors the memory of a person or event

Index

Word Count: 493
Early-Intervention Level: M